Minnie and Moo
and the
Haunted Sweater

Denys Cazet

HarperCollins*Publishers*

For my daughter Michelle,
and for Max and Jerry

HarperCollins®, ☕®, and I Can Read Book® are trademarks of HarperCollins Publishers Inc.

Minnie and Moo and the Haunted Sweater Copyright © 2007 by Denys Cazet All rights reserved.
No part of this book may be used or reproduced in any manner whatsoever without written permission
except in the case of brief quotations embodied in critical articles and reviews. Printed in the United
States of America. For information address HarperCollins Children's Books, a division of
HarperCollins Publishers, 1350 Avenue of the Americas, New York, NY 10019. www.icanread.com

Library of Congress Cataloging-in-Publication Data is available.
ISBN-10: 0-06-073016-1 (trade bdg.) — ISBN-13: 978-0-06-073016-1 (trade bdg.)
ISBN-10: 0-06-073017-X (lib. bdg.) — ISBN-13: 978-0-06-073017-8 (lib. bdg.)

1 2 3 4 5 6 7 8 9 10 ❖   First Edition

Fall Is in the Air

Minnie and Moo

sat under the old oak tree on the hill.

Moo put down her knitting.

"Ahh," she said. "Smell that?

Fall is in the air."

Minnie opened up a pink box.

"Ahh," she said. "Smell that?

Cream puffs are in the wind!"

Moo looked at Minnie.

"What?" said Minnie.

"You said you were on a diet,"
said Moo.

"I am," said Minnie.

"I have twelve cream puffs.

But, because I'm on a diet,

I'm only going to eat eleven."

Moo looked at the farmhouse.

"Today is the farmer's birthday,"
she said.

"You could give the farmer
your last cream puff as a present."

"What a good idea," said Minnie.

"I'll surprise him.

I'll hide it under his pillow."

The Crash

Minnie and Moo walked down the hill

toward the farmer's house.

"I wish I had something

for the farmer," said Moo.

"You'll think of something,"

said Minnie. "You always do!"

A flock of sheep ran past.

"Hey!" said Minnie.

"You better watch where—"

"Out of the way!" someone shouted.

Some chickens ran by carrying Elvis.

"Move it or milk it!" yelled Elvis.

Just as the chickens crossed the road,

the sheep ran in front of them.

"Look out!" cried Elvis.

"Look out!" cried the sheep.

They crashed into one another.

"Oh," moaned the sheep.

"Oh," moaned the chickens.

"Where's Elvis?" Moo asked.

A chicken pointed at the pile of sheep.

"In there!" she sobbed.

Moo pulled on one side of the pile.

Minnie pulled on the other.

"It's no use," said the sheep.

"We're stuck!"

Moo stared at the pile.

"I see something," she said.

"What?" asked Minnie.

"A heap of sheep?"

"No," said Moo. "I see

the farmer's birthday present."

The Farmer's Present

Moo grabbed her knitting needles

and ran back down the hill.

"Moo," said Minnie,

"what are you doing?"

"I'm going to knit the farmer

a new wool sweater," said Moo.

"But what about Elvis?"

asked one of the chickens.

"When I'm finished using the wool,"

said Moo, "the pile will fall apart—"

"Oh!" cried the chickens.

"And there will be our Elvis!"

Moo sat down and began to knit.
She knitted and knitted
until all the sheep were bald.
"There!" she said. "It's done!"

Moo held up the sweater.

"Moo," said Minnie.

"The farmer's new sweater is big.
One sleeve is longer than the other,
and it has a lump in it."

Minnie squeezed the lump.

"ACK!" said the lump.

"Has anyone seen Elvis?"
asked a chicken.

"Shrink It?"

Minnie and Moo

went into the farmer's house.

"Are you sure they're not here?"

Minnie asked.

"They went shopping," said Moo.

Minnie tiptoed into the bedroom

and hid the cream puff.

When Minnie came back,

Moo said, "You're right.

This sweater is much too big!

We need to shrink it."

"Shrink it?" said Minnie. "How?"

"Soak it," said Moo.

"Soak it in warm soapy water!"

Moo put the sweater in the sink.

She turned on the warm water.

Minnie added the soap.

They soaked the sweater.

Then Moo started to squeeze it dry.

"Achoo!" sneezed the sweater.

"OH!" cried Moo.

"What was that?" Minnie asked.

"It was the sweater!" said Moo.

"Moo, don't be silly," said Minnie.

"Sweaters don't sneeze."

Moo grabbed Minnie's arm.

"They do," said Moo,

"if they're haunted!"

The Haunted Sweater

Minnie gasped. "Haunted?"

"Haunted!" said Moo. "Look!"

The sweater began to move.

It crawled across the floor.

It crawled toward Minnie and Moo.

"It's that lump!" said Minnie.

"There's a ghost in there," said Moo.

"It's caught in the sweater.

I must have snagged it

with my knitting needle."

The sweater pointed a sleeve

at Minnie and Moo.

"Yooooou," moaned the sweater.

"Whooo?" Moo asked.

"Mooo," moaned the sweater.

"Mooo?" said Minnie.

"Of course we moo. We're cows."

"YOOOOOU!" shouted the sweater.

"Oh!" gasped Minnie.

"You did this to me!"

said the sweater.

"It was an accident," said Minnie.

"I didn't mean to," said Moo.

The Haunting

Suddenly, the sweater flapped

its sleeves and flew into the air.

"Look out!" cried Moo.

The sweater landed on Moo.

"Get it off! Get it off!" she yelled.

"It's always you two fat cows!"
shouted the sweater.
Minnie grabbed the sweater.
"Don't call my best friend fat!"
she said.

The sweater whacked Minnie

on the head with a wet sleeve.

"You big fat blimp!" said the sweater.

"OH!" Minnie gasped.

Minnie threw down the sweater
and leaped into the air!

Minnie landed on the sweater.

"No one calls me a blimp," she said.

"I'm on a diet!"

"Ow!" said the sweater.

Moo heard the farmer's truck.

"Minnie! Get up!" cried Moo.

"Don't bother me," said Minnie.

"Ghost or no ghost,

I'm teaching this sweater a lesson!"

"Minnie, get up," said Moo.

"The farmer's coming!"

"Out the back door!" cried Minnie.

Happy Birthday

The farmer helped his wife, Millie,

carry shopping bags into the kitchen.

"What's that?" he asked.

Millie picked up the sweater.

"It looks like the wool sweater

I ordered for your birthday,"

she said.

"One sleeve is longer than the other,"
said the farmer. "And it has
a lump in it."
Millie laid the sweater on the table.
"This is new wool," she said.
"It tends to lump up.
I can flatten it with my rolling pin."
"Ohhh," moaned the sweater.

Millie picked up a big pair of scissors.

"This will take care

of the long sleeve," she said.

"ACK!" shouted the sweater.

It jumped off the table

and ran out the door.

The farmer and Millie ran after it.

But the sweater was too fast.

"Oh, dear," Millie said.

"And it was on sale, too."

It's the Thought That Counts

Minnie and Moo

sat under the old oak tree

sipping warm cocoa.

They watched Moo's sweater

running up the hill

toward the chicken coop.

"There goes my present," said Moo.

"And you worked so hard,"
said Minnie.
"That was the best sweater
I've ever knitted," said Moo.
"It's the thought that counts,"
Minnie said.
She poured more cocoa.
"My cream puff
can be from the two of us."
"Thank you," said Moo.

Moo looked at Minnie.

"Minnie," she said. "You didn't really

hide that cream puff

under the farmer's pillow. Did you?"

"Don't be silly," said Minnie.

"I put it where he would find it."

"Where?" Moo asked.

"In his slipper," said Minnie.